THE
CHRISTMAS
EVE TREE

For Ben and Sydell
E.S.

First published 2015 by Walker Books Ltd, 87 Vauxhall Walk, London SE11 5HJ

This edition published 2016

Text © 2015 the Estate of Delia Huddy • Illustrations © 2015 Emily Sutton

www.walker.co.uk • 10 9 8 7 6 5 4 3

THE
CHRISTMAS EVE TREE

written by DELIA HUDDY

illustrated by EMILY SUTTON

WALKER BOOKS
AND SUBSIDIARIES

LONDON · BOSTON · SYDNEY · AUCKLAND

A
forest of
Christmas trees
stretching over the hills.
That's where the story begins.
There the little fir tree was planted,
but planted carelessly
so that when the wind blew strong
it fell sideways on to its neighbour
and had no chance to grow.

The years went by until one December, when the foresters
dug up trees for the Christmas market, the little fir tree,
stunted and still tangled with its neighbour, was loaded
onto a trailer and driven down the motorway
to the city.

"Oh my," it said breathlessly,

for it was at the bottom of the pile.

The tallest trees were unroped

and taken away:

one to stand

proudly in a cathedral;

another in the middle

of a large square;

and a third to decorate the stage at a grand Christmas ball.

But most of the trees were bought by ordinary folk, for houses
where there were children who covered them with stars
and silver tinsel, chocolate mice and small secret parcels.

The little fir tree and its companion were taken to a large store,

where late on Christmas Eve they were the only trees left unsold.

A shopper hurried in to make a last minute purchase.

"You'll not want this weedy thing, miss,"

said the shop assistant, as he pulled the little fir tree

from the roots of the bigger tree and threw it on one side.

The customer smiled and went off, pleased with her buy.

But the little fir tree felt fearful of what its fate might be.

There was a boy in the shop,

drawn in from the rain outside by the warmth and the lights

and the wonderful spicy smell of Christmas.

He said, "You throwing that away? Could I have it?"

The assistant looked at the little fir tree –

hardly what you'd call a tree at all. He shrugged

and handed it over. After all, it was Christmas Eve

and the store would soon be closing.

The boy went outside into the cheerless evening. He held

the little fir tree carefully in front of him so that none

of its few crooked branches would get snapped off by

shoppers on the pavement. He set off on the long walk

to the river. On his way, he found a cardboard box

in a litter bin and took it along too.

When he came to the river,

the tide was out and down the steps

a small pebbly beach was showing.

The boy climbed down and, digging

the mud with his hands,

he planted the little fir tree

in the cardboard box.

Near the steps, under the arches of a railway bridge,

the boy had another cardboard box, big enough to sleep in.

He put the tree on the pavement in front of him.

What a poor thing I am, thought the little fir tree,

but the boy seemed pleased so the little fir tree felt more cheerful.

"I belong to someone now," it said to itself.

And it began to feel like Christmas.

A passer-by dropped a coin into the boy's lap.

It was enough to buy him supper,

but instead he crossed over to the newsagent

and bought some candles and a box of matches.

He fixed the candles to the branches

of the little fir tree.

Now other people were returning

to claim their cardboard boxes for the night.

They gathered round the boy and the little fir tree.

An old busker with an accordion sat down

and soon the notes of a Christmas song

blended with the heavy rumble of the trains overhead.

Everyone started to sing.

More people gathered: home-going travellers, theatregoers,

sightseers. A policeman tried to move them on

but they stood where they were, the singing people,

and the traffic was brought to a halt.

The candles burned steadily

and the old man played and still the people sang.

The little fir tree felt it would burst with happiness,

for it was obvious the boy had forgotten

that tonight he would be sleeping in a cardboard box

under the railway arch, and that tomorrow

he would eat not turkey, but soup in a soup kitchen

if he was lucky.

A few days later the boy moved on.

"You're more dead than alive," he said sadly

to the little fir tree as he went.

And the tree, feeling dry and brittle, had to agree.

But while other Christmas trees

were piled onto January bonfires, the little fir tree

was put in a road sweeper's barrow.

"There's a green shoot here," said the road sweeper,
looking at the tree's roots, and slyly he planted it
in the corner of the park gardens.

There you will find it. Not so little now,
for against all odds it grew – if not big and tall,
at least cheerfully stout.

Now it stretches out its branches for sparrows, pigeons,

babies in prams, lovers and office workers.

Mice nibble its roots.

And as the winter days shorten,

the fir tree dreams of its poor beginnings

in the hills ... of that magical Christmas Eve ...

and of sunny days in the park.

"Who would have thought," it says to itself,

as it looks forward to another spring.